THE CLASSIC

* *

HANS
CHRISTIAN
ANDERSEN

FAIRY TALES

THE CLASSIC

HANS CHRISTIAN ANDERSEN

FAIRY TALES

Retold by Sheila Black

WITH ILLUSTRATIONS BY ERIN AUGENSTINE ❦ ANDREW BABANOVSKY

RICHARD BERNAL ❦ ARLENE KLEMUSHIN ❦ ROBYN OFFICER

KAREN PRITCHETT ❦ RICHARD WALZ

Produced by Ariel Books

COURAGE
BOOKS
AN IMPRINT OF RUNNING PRESS
PHILADELPHIA • LONDON

© 1990 by Armand Eisen, 1997 by Courage Books
All rights reserved under the Pan-American and International
Copyright Conventions.

10 9 8 7 6 5 4 3 2 1
Digit on the right indicates the number of this printing.

Library of Congress Cataloging-in-Publication Number
90-55649

ISBN 0-7624-0185-0

Printed in Singapore
Designed by Michael Hortens
Art direction by Michael Hortens

Front cover illustration by Robyn Officer

Illustrations on pages 11, 12, 14, 15 by Richard Walz
Illustrations on pages 16, 17, 18, 20, 21 by Richard Bernal
Illustrations on pages 22, 23, 48, 49, 50, 51 by Erin Augenstine
Illustrations on pages 24, 25, 26, 27, 28, 29, 52, 53, 54, 56 by Robyn Officer
Illustrations on pages 30, 31, 32, 33 by Karen Pritchett
Illustrations on pages 34, 35, 36, 38, 39, 40, 41 by Arlene Klemushin
Illustrations on pages 42, 43, 44, 46, 47 by Andrew Babanovsky

Published by Courage Books, an imprint of
Running Press Book Publishers
125 South Twenty-second Street
Philadelphia, Pennsylvania 19103-4399

INTRODUCTION

H ans Christian Andersen's life was a kind of fairy tale. Andersen was born in 1805 in Odense, Denmark. His father was a shoemaker and his mother was a washerwoman, and the family had little money. But in spite of poverty and childhood illness, Andersen grew up to become famous. Rather than retelling old folktales as other people had done, Andersen made up his own stories. Today, they are world favorites.

In the imaginary world of Hans Christian Andersen, extraordinary and wonderful things can happen. We can listen as a small fir tree deep in the forest tells us its hopes. A true princess can be bruised by a single pea placed beneath her twelve feather-filled mattresses. And a nightingale's song can save the life of an emperor.

Some of Hans Christian Andersen's stories are happy and some are sad, but all of them are enchanting. For this shoemaker's son, the world was a place of wonder and magic, and so it is for us when we read his tales.

Sheila Black

CONTENTS

THE CLASSIC

HANS
CHRISTIAN
ANDERSEN

FAIRY TALES

THE EMPEROR'S NEW CLOTHES

❧

There was once an emperor who was very vain. He loved new clothes more than anything else and spent all his money on them. He had suits of gold and silver and every kind of silk and satin. He had so many clothes that he wore a different costume every hour of the day.

Now, one day a pair of swindlers came to the city where the emperor lived. They heard how fond he was of clothes, and so they came up with a plan.

They let it be known that they were weavers, and that the fabrics they made were the most wonderful the world had ever seen. Not only were the patterns and colors richer and more beautiful than any others, but these fabrics had magic properties. Clothes made from them would become instantly invisible to anyone who was either a fool or unfit for the office he held.

"What wonderful clothes they must be!" the emperor cried when he heard of them. "I must order some at once!"

The emperor summoned the swindlers to his palace, and gave them a whole chest of gold so that they could begin work immediately.

The swindlers set up large looms. Then they ordered the finest silk and satin threads. But these they hid away in their sacks while day and night they pretended to work the empty looms.

"I wonder how the weaving is going," the emperor said one day. He would have gone to see for himself, but he felt a little strange to think that the cloth would be invisible to anyone who was a fool. So he decided to send his oldest and most trusted minister in his place. "He is very honest and very wise," the emperor said to himself. "Surely he will be able to tell me what the cloth looks like."

And so the old minister went to the room where the two swindlers sat working their looms. But although he opened his eyes as wide as he could, he could see nothing.

"But this is terrible!" he thought. "Can it be that I am really a fool?"

The swindlers smiled and asked him what he thought of the beautiful cloth.

The minister turned bright red. "It is lovely!" he replied. "Indeed, I have never seen anything like it."

Then the swindlers described the cloth in detail, telling the minister of its rich colors and intricate design. The poor man listened closely, so that he would be able to repeat the description to the emperor word for word.

And so the old minister told the emperor how wonderful the magic cloth was, and the emperor sent the swindlers another chest of gold.

Time passed. The emperor decided once again to see how the work was coming along. This time, he sent his most faithful servant in his place.

The faithful old servant went down to the room where the swindlers stood over their empty looms. He peered and peered through his thick spectacles. But no matter how hard he looked, he could see nothing.

"Oh, no!" cried the poor man. "Can it be that I am secretly a fool and not a good servant after all?" The thought was so dreadful that he dared not say that he could not see the cloth at all. And so he, too, listened closely to everything the swindlers said, and went back and told the emperor that the cloth they were weaving was the most amazing stuff he had ever seen.

Now, the emperor decided that he would go see this marvelous cloth for himself. Surrounded by his servants and courtiers, down he went to the room where the swindlers were busy working.

When he came in the swindlers bowed and smiled. They pretended to hold out lengths of their wonderful cloth. Naturally, all of the servants and courtiers dared not admit that they saw nothing. Instead, they all cried at once: "How lovely," and "How original," and "Have you ever seen anything to match it?" Then they insisted that the emperor immediately order a suit made of this wonderful cloth to wear at a great procession that was to take place that very week.

The emperor turned quite pale. He rubbed his eyes. Then he rubbed them again, and he stared and stared. "My goodness!" he said to himself at last. "I can see nothing. Can it be that I am not fit to be emperor?"

But aloud he said only: "What magnificent cloth this is! It is even more wonderful than I dreamed!" Then he ordered that the swindlers be given twenty chests of gold and knighted at once in honor of their great skill.

The day before the procession, the swindlers were seen working around the clock. All night long, candles burned above their looms, and early the next morning they presented themselves before the emperor.

"Your new clothes are ready, sir!" they announced proudly.

Then they led the emperor, along with a great many of his courtiers, to the royal fitting room. There the swindlers made the emperor take off all of his clothes so that he could try on his new suit. When the emperor had undressed, the clever swindlers made him put out his arms so that they could pull on his new shirt and jacket. Then they helped him with his new trousers and, last of all, they pretended to lay a cape with a long train over the emperor's shoulders. Then, they drew back and stared at him in admiration.

"How do my new clothes look?" asked the emperor, turning around in front of the royal mirror. All of his courtiers cried at once: "What colors! What patterns! What fine designs! These are truly the most remarkable clothes you have ever worn!"

Now the procession was ready to begin. Under a scarlet canopy, the

emperor walked into town. The servants who were to carry his train stood behind him lifting up their hands as if they were really holding something, for no one dared say that he could not see the emperor's new clothes!

All along the streets the people gathered. "What beautiful clothes!" they cried. Never had any costume of the emperor's been so admired.

But then a little boy whispered: "But Mother, the emperor has nothing on!"

"Shhh!" his mother cried. But it was too late.

"Did you hear what the child said?" one person whispered to another. "The emperor has nothing on!"

Soon they were all saying it: "The emperor has nothing on!"

The poor emperor turned as red as red can be, for he knew that it was true. But there was nothing he could do about it. So he just kept marching along, and his servants marched behind him, still holding up his invisible train.

And so ends the story of the emperor's new clothes.

THUMBELINA

Once there was a woman who longed for a child, but no child
came. At last she went to see a good fairy who gave her a seed of
barleycorn. "Plant this seed in a flowerpot," she said. "Then see
what happens."

The woman did as she was told. Soon, a beautiful bud with petals of
red and gold sprang up. The woman bent down and kissed it, and the flower
opened wide. Inside sat a beautiful little maiden, no bigger than the
woman's thumb.

The woman was overjoyed. She and her husband named the tiny maiden
Thumbelina, and no child was ever more loved. Her cradle was a walnut shell.
Her blanket was a rose petal, and her pillow was made of violets. At night
Thumbelina slept on the windowsill, and during the day she amused herself by
sailing around a plateful of water on a boat made from a tulip petal.

But one night as Thumbelina slept in her pretty cradle, a big, ugly toad
hopped through the window. When she saw the little maiden, she cried:
"Why, she would make a fine wife for my son!" Then she carried Thumbelina
off to the swampy marsh where she lived with her son.

Her son was even bigger and uglier than she was. When he saw
Thumbelina, he croaked with delight. Thumbelina longed to run away. But
the mother toad placed her on a lily pad in the center of a wide rushing
stream. Here Thumbelina was to be kept prisoner until it was time for
the wedding.

Thumbelina wept, for she did not wish to marry the horrible toad.
Some fish swimming in the stream heard her sob, and when they saw how

beautiful she was, they decided to help her. They gnawed at the stem of the lily pad until they managed to cut right through it, and away sailed Thumbelina downstream.

Soon a big June bug flew by. When he saw Thumbelina, he seized her up in his claws. He thought that she was very beautiful and would make him a fine wife. But when he flew with her to the tree where he lived with all the other June bugs, his friends laughed at him. "You wish to marry her?" they cried. "But she is so ugly! She only has two legs and she has no feelers at all!"

The poor June bug was terribly embarrassed. So he flew Thumbelina down from the tree, and placed her on a daisy in the middle of the forest.

Here Thumbelina lived alone all summer long. She slept on a bed woven out of grass. She ate honey from the flowers, and drank the morning dew. She was happy, for the bright sun was always above her, and the birds sang to her all day long.

But soon autumn came, and then cold winter. The flowers died, and the birds flew away. There was nothing to eat and the wind was so icy that poor Thumbelina almost froze to death.

Off she went, looking for shelter. At last, she came to the home of a field mouse, who lived at the edge of a cornfield. The field mouse had a comfortable house with plenty of food put away. When she saw the pretty maiden, the good field mouse welcomed her inside. "You can stay all winter long if you like," she said "so long as you help me tidy my house, and tell me stories." And so Thumbelina moved in with the field mouse, and the two lived together quite happily.

But one day the field mouse said that she was expecting a visit from her neighbor. "He is very rich and wise," she told Thumbelina. "You must be sure to tell him your prettiest stories, and sing him your nicest songs, for I'm afraid he's quite blind."

The next day the neighbor came, wearing his best black velvet coat. He may have been rich and wise, but Thumbelina did not like him. He was a mole. He lived in a tunnel deep under ground, and had nothing but bad things to say of the sun, the birds, and the flowers that Thumbelina so loved.

Nevertheless, she sang for him. When the mole heard her voice, he fell in love with her. But he said nothing, for like most moles he was very cautious. He merely invited Thumbelina and the field mouse to come visit his home deep under ground. But he said that he would lead them there himself, as there was a dead bird in the passageway and he did not want them to be frightened.

The mole lit a torch and Thumbelina and the field mouse followed him down the long, dark tunnel. When they came to where the dead bird lay, the mole accidentally pushed his nose through the wall of the tunnel, and the sunlight shone in.

In the light, Thumbelina saw that the dead bird was a beautiful swallow. The sight of him made her very sad. She waited until the others had gone ahead. Then she bent over, and kissed the dead bird on the beak. "Thank you for singing to me all summer long," she whispered. Then the field mouse told her to hurry.

That night Thumbelina could not sleep. She kept thinking of the poor swallow. At last, she got up and wove him a thick blanket of soft hay. Quietly, she crept to where he lay, and gently laid the blanket over him. She pressed her head against the swallow's chest when, to her surprise, she heard a loud thumping sound. At first she was frightened, but then she realized that it was only the beating of the swallow's heart. The bird was not really dead at all, but only frozen stiff!

For the rest of the winter Thumbelina nursed the sick swallow with great tenderness. But she was careful not to let the field mouse, or the mole, know what she was up to.

When spring came, the swallow grew well enough to fly away again. He begged Thumbelina to come with him. But she said that she could not leave the field mouse, who had been so kind to her. So, with tears in her eyes, Thumbelina waved goodbye to the swallow.

Spring passed, and then summer. The corn in the field grew so high that it was like a big forest to Thumbelina. Sometimes from the door of the field mouse's house, she stared out at the field, and up at the beautiful blue sky. It made Thumbelina's heart ache, for the field mouse and the mole both hated the sun, and would not let her go outside. Sometimes Thumbelina heard birds sing in the distance, and at such times she missed the beautiful swallow very much.

One day the field mouse told Thumbelina that the mole had asked for her hand in marriage. "But I don't wish to marry him!" Thumbelina cried. "What nonsense!" said the field mouse angrily. "He will make a fine husband!" And she refused to listen to Thumbelina's cries.

Four spiders were hired to weave Thumbelina's wedding gown, and the field mouse busily prepared for the wedding feast.

Thumbelina was very unhappy. She could not imagine marrying the mole. Whenever she could, Thumbelina crept to the door of the field mouse's house. Then she spent hours looking up at the warm, beautiful sun and staring at the birds who flew overhead. "If you ever see the swallow," she called to them, "tell him farewell for me!" Then, one evening, she heard a great burst of song above her, and the swallow himself flew down to meet her.

Thumbelina flung her arms around him and began to weep. She told him how she was to marry the mole and live deep under ground, where she would never see the warm sun or the bright flowers again. "Come with me, instead!" said the swallow, who was flying south for the winter. "You saved my life when I lay in the mole's dark passage, and I have never forgotten it."

And so Thumbelina climbed on the swallow's back, and away they went. They flew over high mountains, fields of golden flowers, and deep green valleys that smelled of oranges. At last, they came to a brilliant blue lake. Beside it stood a palace of gleaming white marble, and on the palace roof were many swallows' nests.

"This is my home," said the swallow. "You would not like it here. But I will place you in the palace gardens, and there you will find all that you need to make you happy."

The swallow set Thumbelina down on a beautiful white flower. The flower opened, and in the center sat a little man—the same size as Thumbelina herself. On his head he wore a gold crown and tiny wings fluttered from his shoulders. He was the angel of the flower; for a tiny spirit lives in every flower, and this little man was the king of them all. As soon as the little king saw Thumbelina, he fell in love with her and asked her to be his wife. Thumbelina said yes. At that, all the flowers in the garden opened. In each one was a tiny man or woman. They flew over to Thumbelina, bearing gifts for their new queen. They gave her many wonderful presents. But best of all was a pair of tiny, gossamer wings that let Thumbelina fly with them from flower to flower. Then the king announced that from that moment on, she would be called Maia.

Then the swallow sang their wedding song, and it was the loveliest song you have ever heard. It was happy and sad, too, for the swallow was bidding farewell to his dear friend Thumbelina, and to the magic land of summer, where the sun never stops shining and the flowers are always in bloom.

THE PRINCESS AND THE PEA

O nce upon a time there lived a handsome young prince. He wanted very much to find a princess with whom to share his kingdom. But he insisted that she be a *real* princess.

He traveled far and wide, and met a great many princesses. Some were slender and some were stout. Some had hair pale as moonlight, while others had hair as black as night. But although he searched high and low, the prince could not find anywhere a princess he wanted to marry. There was something wrong with every one of them. Not a one was a *real* princess.

And so the prince went home to his palace. He was very sad, for he had so wanted to find a real princess!

One night there was a terrible storm. The wind howled, thunder and lightning crashed, and the rain poured down in great sheets. Suddenly, there came a knocking at the palace door. The old king himself went down to answer it.

Standing outside was a princess. She did not look her best, for she was completely soaked. Water streamed from her long golden hair, and her dress was a terrible sight! Nevertheless, she insisted that she was a real princess, and begged for shelter for the night.

The old queen looked the visitor up and down. "I'll soon find out if she's a real princess!" she said to herself, and she welcomed the girl inside.

Then the queen went upstairs to the bedroom. She quickly pulled all the bedclothes from the bed, and placed a single pea in the center of the mattress. She then ordered her servants to fetch twenty feather mattresses, and piled them on top of the pea. Twenty feather beds were piled on top of the mattresses. And right at the very top was where the princess was to sleep.

The next morning, the queen asked, "Did you sleep well?"

"Oh, no!" replied the princess, "It was terrible! I can't imagine what was in the bed, but it was terribly hard and lumpy! I'm afraid I'm black and blue all over!"

As soon as she spoke, everyone saw that she was indeed a real princess. Only a true princess would feel a single pea through twenty mattresses and twenty feather beds!

So the prince, who had fallen in love with her at first sight, immediately asked her to be his bride. The wedding was held that very week. I am happy to say that the princess looked every bit as lovely as a *real* princess should. As for the pea, it was placed in a museum, and for all I know, it is there to this day!

THE STEADFAST
TIN SOLDIER

I n the beginning, there were twenty-four tin soldiers. They first glimpsed the world when a little boy took them out of their box, and set them out on a big table. They had been given to him for his birthday, and he was very proud of them.

All twenty-four wore the most elegant blue and red uniforms, and bravely shouldered their guns. They were all exactly alike, except for the last one. He had only one leg because there hadn't been enough tin to finish him properly. However, he stood up just as straight as the others, for he was a steadfast little soldier.

As soon as he was set out on the table, the tin soldier looked around. There were many things to see. But best of all was a wonderful castle made all out of paper. The castle was so well made that you could look through the windows into the tiny paper rooms. Outside there were little paper trees, and a lake made out of a piece of mirror, on which wax swans swam around in circles. But most beautiful of all was the little dancer who stood in the castle doorway.

She, too, was made all out of paper. But she wore a dress of pale blue gauze with a matching ribbon draped over her shoulders as a shawl. This ribbon was fastened by a silver spangle as big as her whole face. The little dancer's arms were stretched out, and one of her legs was raised so high in the air that the tin soldier could not see it. He decided that she must have only one leg, just like him.

"She would be the perfect wife for me!" he thought. But then he remembered that she lived in a castle, while he had only a tin box which he

24

shared with all of the other soldiers. "She would never agree to marry me!" he told himself. But even so, he could not help staring at her longingly.

He stared at her so hard that he fell over beside a snuff box. But even lying stretched out flat on the table, he continued to keep his eyes on her.

When evening came, the other tin soldiers were put back in their box. Then everyone in the house went to bed. Now was the time when the toys had all their fun. They played all kinds of games. They visited each other, and held splendid balls, and pretended to fight great battles. The poor tin soldiers rattled about in their box, for they longed to join in.

But the soldier and the beautiful paper dancer did not move at all. They only watched each other silently, not taking their eyes off each other for a single moment.

The clock struck twelve, and the lid of the snuff box popped open. But it did not contain snuff at all! Instead, a black goblin—a sort of jack-in-the-box—poked out his head. He noticed the tin soldier staring at the dancer. "Please keep your eyes to yourself!" he said in a nasty voice. The little tin soldier pretended not to hear. "You just wait until tomorrow!" said the wicked black goblin. With that, he disappeared into his box again.

The next morning, the children of the house set the tin soldier on the windowsill. I can't say whether it was because of the wicked goblin, but suddenly a gust of wind blew the window open. The poor tin soldier fell down three stories, head first. He landed between two cobblestones, and it was not a very nice feeling at all.

The little boy went out to look for him. But although he looked and looked, he could not find the soldier anywhere.

Soon it began to rain. The rain fell harder and harder. When it was over, two little boys came walking by.

"Look! There's a fine tin soldier," one of them cried. "Let's make him go for a sail!"

So the boys made a boat out of newspaper, and put the tin soldier inside. Then they sent him sailing down the gutter.

The little paper boat whirled and bobbed all over the place. The tin soldier could not help feeling a little frightened. But as he was a steadfast little soldier, he stood up straight as ever, and shouldered his gun bravely.

Suddenly, the little boat veered down a dark tunnel. "Where am I going now?" wondered the tin soldier. "To think that it is all because of that wicked goblin. If only the little dancer were with me, now! Then, even if it were twice as dark, I should not mind."

The boat rushed quickly through the long, dark tunnel. At last, the little tin soldier could see daylight ahead. His spirits rose. But then he heard a terrible loud, roaring sound. The little paper boat was heading straight toward a great big canal.

The little tin soldier must surely have felt afraid then! The waters of the canal rushed along at such a speed that they were as dangerous for the little tin soldier as an enormous waterfall would be to you or me! But the little tin soldier did not even flinch. Instead, he stood up straighter than ever, and held on to his gun as tightly as he could.

The little boat began to fill up with water. Soon the water came all the way up to the soldier's neck. Then the little paper boat broke in two underneath him.

Down sank the tin soldier. He knew that he was about to die. But still, he thought only of the little dancer. Just as he was about to close his eyes for the last time, a big fish swam up and swallowed him in a single bite!

It was dark and narrow inside the fish's belly. Nevertheless, the little tin soldier managed to hold himself as upright as ever. The fish darted this way and that. Then it became quite still, and a flash like lightning pierced right through it.

"Look, a tin soldier!" someone cried, and the soldier found himself in

daylight again. He was in a kitchen, for the fish had been caught and taken to market. There it had been sold to the cook, who had just cut it open with a big knife.

The cook picked up the tin soldier, and carried him upstairs to the parlor. She wanted to show everyone the brave little man who had traveled about in the belly of a fish. The tin soldier felt a little embarassed by all the fuss. But when the cook put him down on the table he saw, to his amazement, that he was in the very same room he had started out in!

The other tin soldiers were there, and so was the paper castle, with the beautiful dancer still standing in the doorway. The tin soldier stared at her. Her arms were still stretched out, and her leg was still lifted up so high he could not even see it. Like him, she hadn't moved at all from her original position, for she, too, was steadfast.

The little tin soldier was so moved that if he could have, he would have wept tears of tin. But he was a soldier, and soldiers are not supposed to cry. So he only stared at the little dancer, not taking his eyes from her for a single moment. She stared back at him, but neither one said a single word.

At that moment—and this was surely the wicked goblin's doing—one of the little boys picked up the tin soldier and, for no reason at all, tossed him straight into the fire.

The heat felt terrible, but whether it was really the fire, or only the warmth of his feelings, the tin soldier could not say. The bright colors of his uniform soon faded away, and he became gray as lead. But even that might have just been grief.

He looked at the little dancer, and she looked back at him. He could feel himself melting away, but even so he tried to stand up as straight as he could.

Suddenly, the door flew open. The draft caught the little dancer. She fluttered across the room, straight into the fire next to the tin soldier. Then the flames blazed up, and she was gone.

The next morning, when the maid came to clean away the ashes, she found the soldier, melted into the shape of a tin heart. As for the dancer, all that was left of her was her spangle, and that was burned black as coal.

THE FIR TREE

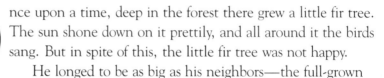

Once upon a time, deep in the forest there grew a little fir tree. The sun shone down on it prettily, and all around it the birds sang. But in spite of this, the little fir tree was not happy.

He longed to be as big as his neighbors—the full-grown spruces and pines. "If I were only as tall as they!" cried the little fir tree. "Then I would be able to see far away into the world!"

Squirrels played in his branches and told him their stories. Wild flowers grew up around him. Sometimes children from town came and played games at his feet. "What a pretty little tree!" they cried. But none of this made the little fir tree happy.

Two winters passed. The little tree grew, but still he cried out, "If only I were tall and old!"

Sunbeams kissed the little fir tree. The dewdrops watered him with their tears. But none of these things pleased him.

Another winter came. Around Christmastime many young trees were cut down. They were loaded onto a wagon, and driven away.

"Some of them are not much taller than I am!" the little fir tree cried. "Where are they going?"

"We know!" sang the sparrows. They told the little fir tree that they had seen trees like them through the windows of the houses in town. The trees were decorated all over with walnuts and sugar candy, the sparrows said. Ribbons and candles were placed in their branches. At night, the candles were all lit. Then people gathered around the trees and sang songs.

"Oh!" cried the fir tree, "I should like that better than anything! Why did they not take me?" And he became more unhappy than ever.

Spring came. Butterflies danced around him. The sunbeams whispered, "Rejoice in your youth!" And the wind sang him lullabyes. But the fir tree paid no attention to these things.

The next winter, the little fir tree was one of the first to be cut down. As the axe sliced through his trunk, he felt pained and afraid. Instead of being happy, he was suddenly sad to be leaving his home in the forest.

The little fir tree was then loaded onto a wagon and driven into town. There, servants in fine costumes carried him into a large and beautiful room. The little fir tree felt quite sick from his journey, and all of his branches trembled. "What is going to happen to me now?" he wondered.

Soon several young ladies came. They draped the little tree with silver and gold paper, and hung walnuts and sugared apples from his branches. Then they fastened candles of white and red all over him, and right at the very top they placed a gold star. "How beautiful the tree will be tonight!" they cried.

"How I wish evening were here!" thought the little fir tree. "I can't wait to see all the candles lit. If only my friends in the forest could see me now!"

At last evening came, and an old man arrived and lit all the candles. The little tree blazed and trembled. The fire frightened him. But he kept very still, for he did not want to harm any of the beautiful ornaments.

A troop of children burst into the room. Their parents and grandparents followed behind them. They gathered under the little fir tree, and danced and sang until the room shook.

"What a lot of noise!" thought the tree. "I wonder if the sparrows from the forest will come to visit me?"

At last, late in the evening, all of the candles had burnt down. Then the children were given permission to take candy from the tree. They sprang upon the little fir tree's branches, pulling him this way and that!

The fir tree was very frightened, but then the children became quiet again. The old man who had lit the candles said that he would tell them the story of Humpty Dumpty. The tree held himself very still, for he wanted to hear the story too. So the little fir tree heard how Humpty Dumpty fell down, and was put together again, and how he then married a princess.

The little fir tree had never heard such a story in his life. "Perhaps I will fall down and marry a princess too," he whispered. But then he became very thoughtful. The house was now quiet and dark, for all of the people had gone to bed. "What will happen now?" wondered the little fir tree. He waited eagerly for the next day to come. He was sure that once again he would be covered with lovely candies and bright candles.

But the next morning when the servants came in, they stripped the little fir tree bare. Then they dragged him down into the cellar, and left him there. The cellar was dark and cold. It was also lonely, and for a long time the fir tree saw no one.

One day, some mice came scurrying across the cellar floor. "Who are you?" they squeaked. "And where are you from?" So the little fir tree told them of his life in the forest. He spoke of the wild flowers, the sunbeams, the squirrels, and the sparrows. The mice had never heard anything like it. "How happy you must have been!" they cried.

"Happy?" asked the fir tree. Then he sighed with all his branches. "Yes, I suppose those were happy days."

Then he told them of the night when he had been decked in candles, and how his branches had been hung all over with walnuts and sugar candies.

The mice thought that this was truly amazing. "How happy you must have been, old fir tree!" they cried.

But the fir tree was insulted, for he did not think that he was old.

"What wonderful stories you tell!" said the mice. And they went and fetched their friends to hear what the fir tree had to say.

So the fir tree told them the story of Humpty Dumpty, which was the only story he knew. The story pleased the mice so much that they told the rats about it. The rats all came to listen too, but they did not like the story nearly as much as the mice did.

"Is that the only story you know?" they asked crossly. "The only one," replied the fir tree. "I heard it on the happiest night of my life, but at the time I did not know that I was happy."

The rats sniffed. "It is a very poor story!" they said. With that they marched off, and the mice followed them.

Now the fir tree was alone again, and he sighed, remembering how much happier he had been when the mice had come to visit him. "Now it is all over," he said to himself. "But I'm sure I will be happy again when I leave this place."

He waited and waited. At last, one morning some servants came and carried the fir tree outside.

How he trembled with joy when he saw the sun shining! "Now I can live again!" he cried, spreading his branches wide. But it was too late. His branches were all withered and yellow. The servants tossed him onto a pile of weeds and nettles. When the fir tree looked around at the grass and the fresh blooming flowers, he felt so sad that he wished he had stayed in the dark cellar.

"If only I had been happy when I lived in the forest," cried the fir tree. "Now it is too late!"

The next day a man came and chopped the fir tree into little pieces. Then he tied them into a bundle, took them inside, and put them in the fireplace.

When the children gathered around the fire, they could hear it sputter and pop. But each popping sound was really the fir tree sighing, and at each sigh he was remembering a scene from his life. He remembered a summer's day in the forest when a soft breeze blew and the sparrows sang. He remembered a clear winter's night when the stars shone icily, and the wind sang a mournful song. And he remembered the candles, and the story he had heard on the happiest night of his life. But soon it was all over, and his story had come to an end, as all stories must.

THE LITTLE MERMAID

Deep down in the depths of the ocean, there once lived a little mermaid. She was the youngest of six sisters and was very beautiful, with eyes as blue as the deepest sea. She lived in a castle of coral with her father, the Sea King. All day long she played with the fishes that passed through, and swam among the purple and red sea anemones that grew along the castle walls.

But unlike her sisters, who were happy in their coral castle, the little mermaid longed, more than anything, to see the world above the sea. She begged her grandmother, whom she loved very much, to tell her all she knew of the ships and towns there. She never tired of hearing that the flowers there had a smell, and that the fish (for so the grandmother called the birds) sang beautiful songs.

Now, all mermaids are allowed to rise to the surface of the ocean in their fifteenth year. The little mermaid was the youngest in her family, so she had the longest to wait. But she listened eagerly when her older sisters came back and told her what they had seen.

The oldest told her of the silvery moon and a town she had seen, its lights glittering like stars. The second described how she had seen the sun setting, making everything look gold. The third was the bravest of all. She swam up a river and rested on a green hill covered with pine trees. The fourth stayed out on the ocean, but she said that it was beautiful, for up there the sea looked like a great bell of glass. The fifth sister went up in the middle of the winter. She saw great icebergs floating by, larger even than the churches built by men. But all five sisters said that they still preferred to remain under the sea in their great coral castle.

The little mermaid listened to their stories, and her
heart was filled with longing. At last, her fifteenth birthday came,
and she was allowed to rise all by herself to the surface of the water.

The sun was just setting when the little mermaid poked her head through
the waves. A large ship all covered with lights was sailing toward her. Music
was playing and people were dancing on the deck. In the middle of them all
was a young prince who was celebrating his sixteenth birthday. He was very
handsome, with large black eyes. As soon as the little mermaid saw him, she
fell in love.

She followed the ship, watching him. The waves grew higher and the
clouds grew dark. A terrible storm was coming and the ship began to rock and
sway. At first the little mermaid thought it was a game, but then she saw that
the people on the ship were frightened. At that moment, a great wave came
and broke the ship apart.

Deep into the water dove the little mermaid, looking for the prince. Her
grandmother had told her that human beings could not live under the water,
and she wished to save him. When she found him, she cradled his head in her
arms, holding him above the water. He was unconscious, and gently she
carried him to land. There she lay him on the beach and kissed him on the
forehead and wished that he might live.

Near the beach was a large white building, and as the sun rose a girl came
out of it. The little mermaid was afraid, and swam out to sea. But she watched
as the girl summoned other people, who came and gathered around the
prince. He opened his eyes and smiled at them, and they led him into the
building. The little mermaid wished that the prince had smiled at her. But she
was hidden among the rocks, and he could not know that it was she who had
saved him.

With a sigh, the little mermaid went back under the water again. But now all of her sisters noticed that she seemed sad and strange. When they asked her what she had seen she would say nothing. Yet whenever she could, she rose to the surface of the water and swam about looking for some sign of the prince. One day she swam up to a great yellow palace with a roof of gold, and there she saw him, standing by the water. After that she followed him whenever she could. More than ever, she longed to live above the water and be like the other human beings she saw.

"If human beings don't drown," she asked her grandmother, "Can they live forever?"

Her grandmother shook her head. "We live three hundred years and they do not even live that long," she said. "But even though they die, they have something we do not have. They have souls which live forever. When we die, we become foam on the surface of the ocean. But they rise up to heaven—a glorious place which we shall never see."

This made the little mermaid more thoughtful than ever. "Could I too get an immortal soul?" she asked.

"Only if a man loved you so much that he held you above all other things, and made you his wife. But that would never happen, for your fish tail, which we consider very beautiful, is thought by human beings to be quite ugly. They think that you must have two legs to be considered handsome."

The little mermaid sighed and looked down at her tail. She thought of the prince and her heart grew sad and still. She thought for a long time. At last, she swam deep down into the water where there lived an old sea witch.

The sea witch was surrounded by sea snakes, and her hair was black as night. "I know why you have come," she told the little mermaid. "And it is very stupid of you. I can give you legs, but let me warn you, at each step you will feel as if you are stepping on sharp knives. And if you want legs, you must give up the loveliest thing you possess—your beautiful voice, for I must cut out your tongue.

"And one more thing," added the sea witch. "If you do not win this man's love you will die on the very day of his wedding, and you will become foam on the surface of the ocean."

The little mermaid trembled, but she thought of the prince and her immortal soul, and she agreed.

So the sea witch cut off her tongue and prepared a magic potion with it. "Drink this tonight when you rise to the surface of the water," she said.

The little mermaid, now unable to speak, swam to the palace of the prince. There she sat upon the marble steps and drank the potion the sea witch had given her. It felt as if a sword had been run straight through her, and she fell into a faint. When she woke up, the prince was standing before her. Looking down, she saw that she now had two legs, just as he did.

The prince asked her who she was and where she came from, but the little mermaid could not answer. Instead, she stared at him sadly with her great blue eyes. He then led her into his palace. Each step she took was like stepping on a sharp knife. Yet she did not complain, but only walked so gracefully that everyone turned to watch her.

The little mermaid soon became the prince's favorite, and he took her with him everywhere. "How I wish you could speak," he cried, "for you are so beautiful and so sad."

As she could no longer sing, she entertained him by performing lovely dances, even though each step hurt her so much that she bled. But although she loved the prince more than life, and he loved her, to her sorrow he never thought of her as a wife.

One day, it was announced that the prince was to be married to a princess from a neighboring kingdom. "I would rather marry you than this princess I am supposed to meet," the prince told her. "I love you best, for you remind me of the girl who saved my life once, and I have never seen her again."

The little mermaid stared at him sorrowfully, for she could not tell him that it was she who had saved him.

And so they sailed to the neighboring kingdom. The princess was waiting at the harbor to meet them. She was very beautiful, with deep blue eyes like those of the little mermaid. When the prince saw her, he threw his arms around her. "It was you who saved my life!" he cried, and announced that she would be his bride.

The little mermaid kissed his hand, but her heart felt as if it were breaking. His wedding morning would bring death to her. Yet still she smiled and watched him with her sad eyes.

The wedding day came. In the great church, the prince and the princess were joined together forever. The little mermaid held the princess' train, but her eyes were distant, for she could think only of the night of death before her.

That evening the prince and his princess boarded the ship that would take them back to his kingdom. The ship set sail, and in the night, when the prince and princess had retired, the little mermaid went up on deck and stared out across the water.

Suddenly, she saw her five sisters rising up out of the water. But their beautiful long hair no longer flowed around them. "We have given our hair to the sea witch," they cried, "to help you so that you won't die tonight." They handed her a knife. "If you plunge this knife into the heart of the prince before sunrise, you can come back to the sea and live out your three hundred years. His life for yours, but act quickly, for there is not much time." With sad smiles, her sisters vanished beneath the waves, leaving the little mermaid holding the magic knife.

Silently, the little mermaid stepped into the prince's cabin. She looked down at him asleep with his princess, and her heart seemed to break all over again. She held the knife and her hand trembled. Then she flung it away from her into the waves. Where it landed, the water turned red as blood. Then the little mermaid looked one more time at the prince she loved, and flung herself after it.

She felt her body dissolving and was sure she was dying. Suddenly she found herself in bright sunlight, and hundreds of beautiful clear beings floated around her. "Where am I?" she cried. "Among the daughters of the air!" came the answer. "A mermaid has no immortal soul and can only attain one through the love of a human being. But daughters of the air, while they do not have a soul, can gain one through good deeds. We fly around the world and soothe mortal sorrow. We are the cool breeze on a blistering hot day. We carry the perfume of the flowers from place to place. You, poor little mermaid, have through your goodness and suffering made yourself into one of us. Now you can someday win for yourself a soul.

When the little mermaid heard this, her eyes filled with tears. She looked down and saw the prince and his bride standing on the deck of the ship. They were searching the waves with sad eyes, as if they knew that she had thrown herself there. Swooping down, the little mermaid kissed the prince's forehead one last time, and then rose with the other spirits of the air high up into the clouds.

THE NIGHTINGALE

There was once a Chinese emperor whose palace was the most beautiful in the world. It was made out of the finest porcelain, and was so fragile that you could only touch it with the greatest care. All around the palace were gardens filled with the rarest flowers. The loveliest of these flowers had silver bells tied to them, which tinkled day and night. Past the gardens there were deep blue lakes, and lofty woods that stretched all the way to the sea. In these woods there lived a nightingale. This nightingale sang so beautifully that fishermen busy casting their nets always stopped to listen to him, and felt glad inside when they heard his song.

Travelers from all over the world came to visit the emperor. They all admired his porcelain palace and his splendid gardens. But when they heard the nightingale, they all said, "This is best of all."

Some wrote books about the emperor's kingdom. They described his palace and his gardens. But most of all they wrote about the nightingale. And so it was that the emperor first heard of the bird.

"What is this?" he cried. "Why is it that I have never heard of this nightingale?"

He summoned all his courtiers and wise men and asked them about the nightingale. But no one at court had ever heard of the bird, except for one person—a lowly kitchen maid. She said, "Ah, yes, the nightingale! Every night when I walk to the sea to bring food for my poor sick mother, I hear his song. It always brings tears to my eyes, for it is as if my mother herself were kissing me."

When he heard this, the emperor immediately sent out a party of his courtiers to order the bird to come and sing before the court. Led by the kitchen maid, they walked across the gardens and into the woods.

A cow began to bellow in the distance. "Oh!" cried one lady-in-waiting. "What a powerful sound. That must be the nightingale! Who would think that he could make so much noise?"

"Oh no," said the kitchen maid. "That is just a cow. We still have a long way to go."

Some frogs began croaking in the marsh. "How beautiful!" cried a courtier. "The nightingale's song sounds like church bells!"

"Oh, no! Those are just frogs," replied the kitchen maid with a smile, "but I think we will hear the nightingale soon."

Just then, beautiful warbling music filled the air. It was the nightingale's song.

"How charming!" the courtiers cried. But when they saw the nightingale perched on a branch above them, they were quite disappointed. "He is so gray and common looking," whispered one lady-in-waiting. "Not at all what I expected." Nevertheless, they invited the nightingale to come to the palace to sing for the emperor that very evening.

"My song sounds best among the trees," the nightingale replied. "But I will be glad to come."

That night the court gathered to wait for the nightingale. They were all wearing their finest silks and satins. In the center sat the emperor on his throne, dressed all in gold.

At last, the little gray bird appeared and began to sing. His song was as lovely as the woods on a quiet evening when twilight fills the air with blue shadows. Everyone grew quiet. When the nightingale finished his song, tears glistened on the emperor's cheeks. He announced that he would give the nightingale the gold slipper that he wore around his neck. But the little gray bird refused. "I have seen tears in the eyes of the emperor," he said. "And that is reward enough."

After that, the nightingale was asked to stay at court and sing for the emperor every night. A cage of pure gold was made for him, and a gold rod for him to perch on. And everyone in court said that his song was surely the most beautiful in the world.

But one day a parcel arrived for the emperor from the emperor of Japan. When the Chinese emperor opened it, he found a nightingale inside made all of gold, and studded all over with precious jewels. On a ribbon tied around its neck was written: "The Emperor of Japan's nightingale is nothing to the Emperor of China's."

"How beautiful it is!" everyone at court exclaimed. They grew even more excited when they found that they could wind up the gold bird and make it sing.

"The real nightingale must sing with the new one!" they cried. But that did not go well. The artificial nightingale sang the same song over and over again, whereas the real nightingale sang differently each time. After they had finished, everyone said that the artificial nightingale should sing on its own. They listened, clapping as it sang the same tune—a waltz—thirty times over. "How wonderful!" they cried. "And it is so much prettier than the real bird."

But the emperor said that they must now let the real nightingale sing alone. When the courtiers and ladies-in-waiting looked around, however, they found that the little bird had flown away.

"How ungrateful!" they cried. They all agreed that the artificial nightingale was much better, and sang better too. And so the real nightingale was banished from the kingdom, and no one was allowed to speak of him.

In his place, the artificial nightingale was placed in a gold cage beside the emperor's bed. Every night, the court gathered to hear it sing. Things went on this way for a year. Then, one day the gold bird opened its mouth, and nothing came out but an ugly whirring sound. Jewelers worked to repair the golden bird, but after that the artificial nightingale could only sing once a year.

Five years passed, and a great sadness fell upon the kingdom. The emperor was very ill, and was expected to die. Pale and still, he lay on his great golden bed with the gold nightingale beside him. Doctors came and went, but nothing could be done.

The emperor could hardly breathe. When he opened his eyes, he seemed to see the figure of Death standing on his chest and wearing his gold crown. The room seemed very still. "Music!" cried the emperor, "If only I could have music!" He turned to the gold bird in its cage. "Sing!" he begged it. "I have given you my gold slipper. I have given you a place of honor beside me. Now, please sing!" But of course there was no one to wind it up, and the golden nightingale remained silent. The room grew cold as ice, and from the corner Death fixed his great silent eyes on the emperor.

Suddenly, from the window there came a burst of song. It was the living nightingale perched on a branch outside. His song swelled through the room. It was so lovely that even the face of Death grew soft, and he opened his thin gray lips, and begged the bird to go on.

As the emperor listened, the nightingale sang of the woods in the morning when the sun is rising, and of quiet churchyards where roses bloom. He sang of the lofty mountains at sunset, and of the deep blue of the night. He sang so beautifully that the emperor felt himself stir back to life, and grim Death felt a longing to die himself and, like a cold gray mist, slipped out the window and was gone.

"Thank you, nightingale!" cried the emperor. "I banished you from my kingdom. Yet you came back, and saved my life. How can I ever repay you?"

"The first time I ever sang for you," the nightingale replied, "I saw tears in your eyes, and I will never forget it. Those tears were all the reward I need."

Pffft! The match flared up with a strong, warm light. Eagerly, she cupped her hands around it. But then a strange thing happened. The light of the match blazed up all around her. It seemed as if she were sitting in front of a stove made out of gleaming brass. A beautiful fire blazed inside it, warming her all over. But just when she felt that she was stretching out her feet toward it, the match went out. The big stove and the beautiful fire vanished, and she was left holding only a burnt matchstick in her hand.

She struck another one. It blazed up, and where the light shone on the wall, the stone became as transparent as glass. It seemed to the little girl as if she could see straight through the wall into a beautiful room. There she saw a table spread with a snow-white tablecloth and covered all over with fine china. In the center a steaming roast goose stuffed with apples lay on a platter. And what was even more wonderful was that the goose suddenly hopped off its dish, the carving knife still stuck in its back, and waddled across the floor toward her. But when the goose drew close, the match went out. The little girl once again found herself staring at the cold stone wall.

Eagerly she lit a third match. This time she was sitting under a great Christmas tree—much bigger and more beautiful even than the ones she had glimpsed through rich men's windows that Christmas. The tree seemed to stretch right up to the sky. It was covered all over with flickering candles. Around it were all sorts of colored pictures such as she had sometimes seen in shop windows. These pictures were so bright that they seemed almost alive. But when the little girl reached out to touch them, out went the match. The pictures vanished, and all of the candles on the Christmas tree seemed to rise higher and higher until the little girl saw that they were only the stars, twinkling far above. One of them fell, making a bright streak of light across the sky.

THE
LITTLE MATCH
GIRL

Late one cold New Year's Eve a little girl wandered the dark, frozen streets. Although it was snowing, she wore no hat and no shoes. Her little feet were blue with cold, but she paid no attention to that. Instead, she peered up at all the lighted windows, and sniffed at the delicious smell of roast goose that was coming from all of the houses. Everyone else was sitting down to eat their New Year's Eve feast, but the little girl had nowhere to go.

Her apron was full of matches, and she carried a packet of them in her hand. All day long she had been trying to sell them, but nobody had bought a single one. Now it was very late, and the little girl was so cold that she could hardly move.

Great white snowflakes fell down on her golden hair and dotted her eyelashes. Too tired to brush them off, she walked slowly up and down the empty streets looking for a place to rest. At last she came to a corner between two houses that was sheltered from the wind. There she sat down, pulling her feet up under her. But she only felt colder than ever.

She was afraid to go home because she had not sold a single match. Her father would probably beat her. Besides, at home it was almost as cold as it was outside, for the walls were full of cracks where the wind came howling through day and night.

Her poor hands were stiff with cold. She looked down at the pile of matches in her apron. How much warmer she would feel if only she dared light one! A single match would do so much good! Trembling, she pulled one out and struck it against the wall.

With that, the nightingale sang for the emperor again until he felt rested and well.

"Please stay with me," said the emperor. "Please stay with me and sing for me always."

"I have done all the good I can," said the nightingale. "Now I must go back to the woods, for I am not happy living in a palace. But do not worry. Every evening I will perch outside your window and sing for you. I will cheer you up, and make you think, too. I will sing of good things and of bad. I will sing of happy things, and of things to make you cry. In my songs, you will hear of everyone in your kindgom—great lords and humble fishermen, proud ladies and poor serving maids." Then the nightingale sang the emperor to sleep.

The next morning, the courtiers gathered to bid farewell to their emperor. They were sure that he had died in the night. How astonished they were when, instead, he came walking toward them and said, "Good morning!"

"Someone must be dying," said the little girl, for her grandmother, who was the only person who had ever truly loved her, had once told her that whenever a star falls, a soul is going up to heaven.

She struck another match. This time it was her grandmother who appeared in the circle of flame. She looked so peaceful and happy that the little girl could hardly bear it.

"Oh Grandmother!" she cried. "Please take me with you. I know you will vanish just like the warm stove, the delicious goose, and the beautiful Christmas tree! Please take me with you!"

Quickly, she struck as many matches as she could, for she so wanted to keep her grandmother beside her.

Their light flared up, making the dark corner as bright as day. As the little girl watched, her grandmother again appeared before her. Never had she looked so gentle and beautiful. The little girl reached out her arms, and her grandmother lifted her up. Together, they rose high into the sky, far above the town with its dark, icy streets. They went to a place where there was no cold and no hunger—for the little match girl and her grandmother rose all the way to heaven.

The next morning, some passersby found the little girl sitting in the corner between the two houses. Her cheeks were rosy, and there was a smile on her lips. But she was dead, frozen to death on the last night of the year. In her apron was a pile of burnt matchsticks. "The poor child," they cried. "Look! She must have tried to warm herself!" But they could not know what beautiful visions the little girl had seen, nor how joyfully she had entered the New Year with her grandmother in a blinding halo of light.

THE UGLY DUCKLING

One fine summer's day next to a quiet pond, a mother duck sat on her nest. She had been sitting there a long time and was getting tired. Then the eggs began to hatch.

"Crack!" they went, one after the other. All the little ducklings poked their heads out. The mother duck was delighted. But then she saw that one egg had not hatched.

It was a very odd-looking egg. It was gray and much larger than the others.

"That's not a duck's egg at all," the other ducks cried when they saw it. "It's a turkey's egg. You've been tricked. Just leave it. There's no point in sitting on an egg like that!"

But the mother duck said that she had been sitting on the egg for so long that she might as well wait a little longer. So she sat very still and, at last, the big egg slowly cracked open.

Out tumbled the last little duckling. But what a strange duckling he was! He was twice as big as any of the others, and not a pretty yellow color, but a dirty gray all over.

"How ugly he is," all the other ducklings cried. But their mother quickly hushed them up. "I don't think he's so ugly," she said. "And look!" she cried, watching as the ugly duckling went splashing into the pond. "He certainly knows how to swim!"

The other ducks in the duck yard stared at the ugly duckling. It was true that he *was* a good swimmer, but he was still the ugliest duckling they had ever seen!

Soon everyone in the duck yard made fun of him. His brothers and sisters

The ugly duckling swam slowly toward the great swans. When he drew near them, he bent his head and waited for their attack, for he was ready to die.

But when the swans reached the ugly duckling, they only circled around him welcomingly. And looking down into the still water, the ugly duckling suddenly saw his own reflection.

He was no longer gray and ugly, but had a long, graceful neck like the others, and feathers of pure white. The ugly duckling had grown into a beautiful swan!

Some little children came running to the edge of the lake. "Look!" they cried, pointing at the swans. "There's a new one! Why, he's the prettiest of all!"

When he heard them the new swan became quite shy, and hid his head under his wing. The children's praise did not make him proud. He had a good heart, and remembered how everyone had once scorned him. "How lucky I am!" he thought to himself. "And to think, I never dreamed I would be so happy when I was the ugly duckling!"

"You are very ugly," clucked the hen disapprovingly. "Can you really lay eggs?"

The duckling shook his head shyly. "No."

"Can you arch your back and purr?" asked the cat.

The ugly duckling shook his head again.

"Then what good are you?" said the cat.

"What good indeed!" cried the hen.

With that they turned their backs on the ugly duckling. After that the big gray cat scratched him and the hen pecked him, and when the old woman found out that he couldn't lay eggs, she kicked him with her big heavy boots. So the ugly duckling set out again.

It was autumn, and the leaves fell from the trees. Now the ugly duckling was all alone. During the day he swam in rivers and lakes. At night he slept among the tall grasses.

Winter came, and all the rivers and lakes froze over. Because the ugly duckling could no longer swim, he passed his days staring up at the sky.

One evening, he saw flying above him the most beautiful birds he had ever seen. They were pure white with long, waving necks. As they flew they made an odd sound—a piercing cry that filled the ugly duckling with a strange joy. He stared up at the beautiful birds for as long as he could. But they soon vanished, for they were swans flying south for the winter.

It grew colder, and snow fell. The ugly duckling hid in the tall grass, and saw no one. Often he thought of the great white birds he had seen flying south. Such beautiful creatures must surely be happy! It would be too sad to tell of all the hardships the ugly duckling suffered during that long, hard winter. Many times, he almost died of the cold. One day a peasant found him lying frozen stiff on the ice. The peasant took him home, but when his children saw the ugly creature they burst out laughing, and chased him away again.

But one day the sun began to shine warmly again. Birds sang in the trees, and the hedges sprouted tiny new green leaves. Spring had come.

The ugly duckling stretched out his wings. To his surprise, he found that they were much stronger than before. He flapped and flapped until he rose high into the air.

Soon he came to a beautiful green garden. In front of him was a sparkling blue lake. There, coming toward him across the water, were three swans.

When the ugly duckling saw the proud birds, he felt as if his heart would break. "I will swim toward them!" he said to himself. "They will surely kill me because I am so ugly. But better to be killed by these beautiful creatures, than endlessly pecked at by ducks and hens, and hated by everyone!"

bit him and pushed him when their mother wasn't looking. The older ducks ignored him, and the younger ones kicked at him and pecked at him whenever he came too close.

"If only the cat would catch you and eat you up!" his brothers and sisters cried. At last even his mother grew tired of defending him. "If only I had never set eyes on you!" she sighed.

"Everyone hates me because I am so ugly!" the poor ugly duckling whispered to himself. And so he decided to leave the duck yard and go out into the big wide world.

He soon came across some wild geese. They stared at him curiously. "You are very ugly," they said, "but you seem harmless enough." And they invited him to come live with them in their home in the marsh.

The ugly duckling happily agreed.

But as soon as they reached the marsh, some hunters came and shot at the wild geese with their guns. They all fell down dead, staining the marsh water red as blood. The ugly duckling hid in terror. A pack of dogs came running through the grass, but they paid no attention to him. "I am too ugly for them to even bite!" the ugly duckling thought sadly. Then he fled into the woods.

When night fell, he came to a little cottage. An old woman lived there with a big gray cat and a red hen. The hen laid fresh eggs every morning.

The old woman's eyes were not very good, and when she saw the ugly duckling, she thought that he was a big fat duck who had escaped from the duck yard. "Now, I'll have fresh duck eggs every morning!" she said happily. And so she welcomed the ugly duckling inside. The cat and the hen studied their visitor curiously.